Things Tha

Contents

What Can Sting?

Many different animals can sting.

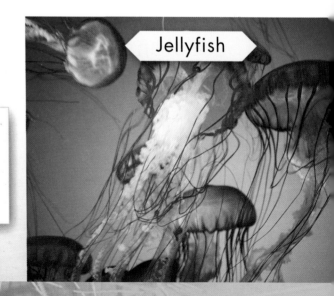

Jellyfish

Having a stinger can protect an animal and help it catch food.

Stingray

Scorpion

Bee

Lionfish

3

Bees

This bee can sting.
It has a stinger
at the end of its body.

A bee's stinger

5

Jellyfish

These jellyfish can sting.
They have stingers
on their tentacles.

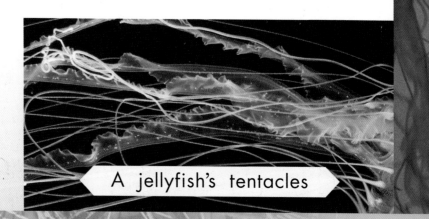

A jellyfish's tentacles

7

Scorpions

This scorpion can sting.
It has a stinger
on the tip of its tail.

A scorpion's stinger

Lionfish

This lionfish can sting.
It has stingers
on its fins.

A lionfish's stingers

Stingrays

This stingray can sting.
It has a stinger
on the top of its tail.

A stingray's stinger

What Else Can Sting?

These animals can sting, too.

Wasp

Io caterpillar

Stonefish

Index